Harry Goes To Day Camp

For Camp Greylock

PUFFIN BOOKS
Published by the Penguin Group
Penguin Books USA Inc., 375 Hudson Street, New York, New York 10014, U.S.A.
Penguin Books Ltd, 27 Wrights Lane, London W8 5TZ, England
Penguin Books Australia Ltd, Ringwood, Victoria, Australia
Penguin Books Canada Ltd, 10 Alcorn Avenue, Toronto, Ontario, Canada M4V 3B2
Penguin Books (N.Z.) Ltd, 182-190 Wairau Road, Auckland 10, New Zealand

Penguin Books Ltd, Registered Offices: Harmondsworth, Middlesex, England

First published in the United States of America by Viking Penguin,
a division of Penguin Books USA Inc., 1990
Simultaneously published in Puffin Books
Published in a Puffin Easy-to-Read edition, 1994

7 9 10 8 6

The Library of Congress has cataloged the Viking Penguin edition under the catalog card number 89-62905.
Puffin Easy-to-Read ISBN 0-14-037000-5

Printed in the United States of America

Reading Level 1.5

Harry Goes To Day Camp

James Ziefert
Pictures by Mavis Smith

PUFFIN BOOKS

“The bus is here!
The bus is here!”
said Harry’s mother.

Harry took his camp bag.
He took his lunch bag.
And he ran out the door.

Harry got on the bus.
He found a good seat.
He was off to camp!

Everybody on the bus sang:
99 bottles of beer on the wall
99 bottles of beer
If one of the bottles should happen to fall…

98 bottles of beer on the wall
98 bottles of beer...
If one of the bottles
should happen to fall...

97 bottles of beer on the wall
96 bottles...95 bottles...
94 bottles...93 bottles...
92 bottles...91 bottles...

“We’re at camp!”
said the bus counselor.
“Everybody off!
And take your stuff!”

Harry found his group.
He found his counselor.

He gave his lunch
to his counselor.

He put his bag
in his cubby.

“What do we play first?”
Harry asked.
“Soccer,” said the counselor.

"Aww! Soccer!" Harry whined.
"When do we go swimming?"
"Later," said the counselor.

Harry played soccer.

Harry played...

but not very well!

"What do we play next?"
Harry asked.
"Basketball," said the counselor.

"Aww! Basketball!" Harry whined. "When do we go swimming?"
"Later," said the counselor.

Harry played basketball.

Harry played...

but not very well!

It was time for lunch.
Harry liked lunch.
He ate everything.
And he drank his milk.

"When do we go swimming?"
Harry asked.
"Later," said the counselor.
"After lunch we rest."

Harry rested.
He rested on his mat.
He rested until he heard,
"It's time for swimming!"

"Hey! Hey!" Harry yelled.
"Let's go!"

Harry was the first one ready.

Harry jumped into the pool.
He made a big splash!

Harry was a great swimmer.

He swam with his head
out of the water.

He swam with his head
in the water.

He floated on top of the water.

He paddled under the water.

And he raced!

"Harry is the winner!"
yelled the counselor.
"Hooray for him!
Everybody out of the water!"

NO
NO
NO
4 FT

Harry's counselor said,
"It's time for music."

"Aww!" said Harry.
"When do we go swimming?"